UP FOR THE CUP

Alan Durant got the football bug at the age of eight and has never looked back. He supports Manchester United and his favourite player of all time is George Best. Among his many books for children are *Creepe Hall, Return to Creepe Hall, Jake's Magic, Spider McDrew, Happy Birthday, Spider McDrew, The Fantastic Football Fun Book* and the picture books *Big Fish Little Fish* and *Angus Rides the Goods Train*. He also writes novels and mystery stories for older children. Alan lives south of London with his wife, three young children, cat and a garden shed in which he does his writing. He hopes one day to be able to fully understand the offside rule.

Titles in the **Leggs United** series

1
THE PHANTOM FOOTBALLER
2
FAIR PLAY OR FOUL?
3
UP FOR THE CUP
4
SPOT THE BALL
5
RED CARD FOR THE REF
6
TEAM ON TOUR
7
SICK AS A PARROT
8
SUPER SUB

All **Leggs United** titles can be ordered at your local bookshop or are available by post from Book Service by Post (tel: 01624 675137).

UP FOR THE CUP

ALAN DURANT

ILLUSTRATED BY
CHRIS SMEDLEY

MACMILLAN CHILDREN'S BOOKS

First published 1998 by Macmillan Children's Books
a division of Macmillan Publishers Limited
25 Eccleston Place, London SW1W 9NF
Basingstoke and Oxford
www.macmillan.co.uk
Associated companies throughout the world

ISBN 0 330 35128 1

3 5 7 9 8 6 4

A CIP catalogue record for this book is available from
the British Library.

Typeset in Baskerville BE
Printed and bound in Great Britain by Mackays of Chatham plc, Kent

LEGGS UNITED

FAMILY TREE

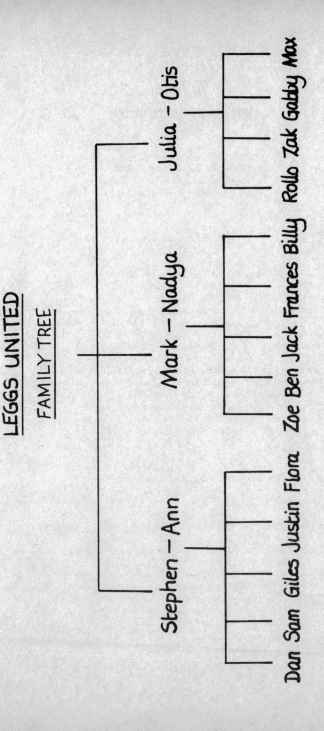

To Josie,
my great entertainer

Chapter One
EXCITING NEWS

"Tottenham!" Sam Legg screeched. "We've drawn Tottenham Hotspur! At home!" She danced about the sitting room as if her team, Muddington Rovers, had *won* the cup rather than just being drawn against a top Premier League team in round three.

Her older brother, Dan Legg, was excited too. He sat on the sofa with a broad grin on his round, freckly face. "Tottenham Hotspur, at home," he repeated dreamily. It seemed almost too good to be true. Suddenly, his grin slipped into an anxious frown. "Do you think we'll get tickets?" he said, tugging at his ear.

"You bet!" declared Sam. "I wouldn't miss this match for the world." She tossed her head emphatically. "Anyway," she added, "Dad says that people who turn up to support regularly go to the front of the queue for cup tickets."

Sam and Dan often went to see Muddington Rovers play. Usually they went with their dad, Stephen Legg, and their younger twin brothers, Giles and Justin. Sometimes their cousin Zak Browne, Dan's best friend, went too. He lived in the same street as Sam and Dan; a third set of cousins lived in the house next door to them. The children of all three families were football mad and had formed a team called Leggs United.

"We'll have to get Archie to come too," said Sam, running her hand over her short red hair.

"Yeah, well, it's easy for him, isn't it?" said Dan. "He doesn't need a ticket."

Archie, alias Archibald Legg, was the

2

children's great-great-uncle, deceased. He had once been a player for Muddington Rovers, but, after being struck down by lightning, he had become a ghost. For over sixty years, he had been trapped inside an old ball in the Leggs' loft, until, quite by chance, Sam and Dan had released him. Now he was the manager of Leggs United.

"Let's call him up and tell him the great news," said Sam.

"Good idea," Dan agreed.

The two children went over to the glass-fronted cabinet which housed the old football, flanked by a pair of ancient leather shin-guards. Sam lifted the ball out and started to rub it gently. Then, as if she were Aladdin summoning the genie from his magic lamp, she wailed, "Archie. Arise, O Archie!"

Her words had an immediate and dramatic effect. There was a fizz and a flash and a ghostly figure whooshed out of the ball into the room. He stood, shimmering and sparkling from head to toe like tinsel on a Christmas tree.

For a moment, the two children stared at the phantom footballer, taking in the knotted red neckerchief, the old black and green striped Muddington Rovers shirt, the long, baggy, white shorts, the thick green socks that concealed bulky shin-pads and the clumpy leather football boots with steel toecaps. As ever, Archie's skin was almost transparently pale and contrasted with the bright red of his bushy caterpillar eyebrows, enormous walrus moustache and flaming shock of hair. Around him there was a ghostly glow.

"Mmm, I feel in fine fettle," he announced, with an extravagant waggle of his moustache. "That new contraption of your mother's is really most invigorating."

"Eh?" Dan uttered, puzzled.

"Archie charged himself up on Mum's new sewing machine," Sam explained, giggling. "Mum was making one of her dresses at the time, right. Suddenly the machine went completely crazy and Mum stitched the dress material to the sleeve of her jumper. She was really mad."

"Yes, well, just a minor accident," Archie burbled. "These things happen with electricity." Archie had discovered that if he focused on something electrical, it boosted his ghostly energy. Right now he was ablaze with it. "In my day, of course," he went on, "we relied a lot more on gas. Gas, you know, is far more dependable . . ."

Dan quickly interrupted before Archie could launch into one of his lectures about the old days. "Archie, we've got something important to tell you," he cried. "Muddington Rovers have drawn Tottenham Hotspur in the cup!"

Archie showed no excitement. In fact, he met the news with a look of cool disdain. "Tottenham, eh?" he sniffed. "Well, Muddington should make mincemeat of a minor team like that."

Sam and Dan stared at Archie once more, this time in total astonishment.

"Tottenham aren't minor," said Dan at last. "They're one of the biggest clubs in the country."

Now it was Archie's turn to show astonishment. "Tottenham, a big club?" he queried. "Why, in my day, they were a very minor outfit indeed. They weren't even in the top division." He paused an instant, raising his thick eyebrows. "But then, of course, in my day every club was minor compared to the great Herbert Chapman's Arsenal."

Sam and Dan looked at one another and rolled their eyes. Archie was always going on about the Arsenal side of the 1930s and its manager, Herbert Chapman. If he'd mentioned them once, he'd mentioned them a thousand times.

"Well, anyway, Archie," Dan said, changing the subject back to the present, "Tottenham are a very big team now."

"But Muddington Rovers are still going to beat them," said Sam with a defiant toss of her head. "Tommy Banks will tear them apart."

"Mmm, well, strange things happen in the cup, laddy," Archie stated calmly. Usually Sam corrected Archie when he

called her "laddy", but right now she was too busy dreaming of her hero, Tommy Banks, Muddington Rovers' star striker. "Tell me," continued Archie, "when is this great match to take place?"

"The day after our cup match against Amberley Park," Dan informed his ghostly relative. The cup in question was the Muddington District Junior Cup. Amberley Park were Leggs United's opponents in the first round.

"We'll thrash them," Sam chirped and she started dancing around the room again.

Archie shook his head and sighed.

Chapter Two

MOUNTAINS AND MOLEHILLS

On Friday, the following week, Dan came back from school with exciting news.

"I'm going to the match!" he cried, bursting into the kitchen, where his family were about to eat their tea.

"That's nice, dear," said Ann Legg, putting a plate of hot crumpets on the table. "Which match is that?"

"The cup match!" Dan exclaimed. "Muddington against Tottenham. We're going to be guests of honour. Mr Barnard said."

Mr Barnard was the teacher in charge of Muddington Primary's school football team. At the end of football practice that afternoon, as Dan now explained, he had given his team the news that they had all been invited to the cup match against Tottenham. They were going as the special guests of Muddington Rovers' new chairman, who was an old boy of Muddington Primary. They'd watch the game from the hospitality seats in the central stand and be introduced to all the players.

"You lucky devil," said Sam enviously. Her green eyes narrowed in a grumpy glare. "It's not fair. I should go too."

"But you're not in the team," Dan reminded her.

"I ought to be," Sam grumbled. It was a rule at Muddington Primary that only children in the top class could play for the school team.

"Well, you will be next year," said Ann Legg soothingly.

"But that's no good, is it?" Sam

complained. "I want to be in the team now and meet the Muddington players with Dan and Zak and Zoe." Zak Browne and Zoe Legg were both in the top class like Dan and played for the school team.

"I'll get you Tommy Banks's autograph," Dan offered.

But Sam was not pacified. "Hmph," she grunted, wrinkling her small nose disgustedly.

She was still sulking the next day when Leggs United gathered for their Saturday morning training session with Archie. There were a couple of things he wanted to sort out before their league match that afternoon against Marchmont Road Juniors.

It was Leggs United's first ever season in the Muddington Junior League, a local football league for under-twelves. So far they were doing well and had won most of their matches. They'd already played Marchmont Road Juniors away and beaten them, so they expected to win the return game at home.

Leggs United's home ground was a

meadow, at the bottom of the gardens of
No. 15 and No. 17 Poplar Street, owned by
the Legg family. They played all their home
matches there and they trained there too.
The meadow had been turned into a
football pitch during the last week of the
summer holidays by the Leggs and Brownes
themselves – under the critical eye of
Archie. The phantom coach was always
quick to point out any fault he found with
the playing surface.

He was standing now in the centre circle,

frowning at a bump on the pitch. It looked suspiciously like a molehill.

"Moles," he tutted. "What confounded creatures they are."

His remark drew an immediate reaction from Sam. "I think they're nice," she retorted fiercely.

"Only because they're small and chubby and they remind you of Tommy Banks," teased Dan.

Sam gave her older brother a scorching look.

"Tommy Banks isn't small or chubby," she hissed. "He's well built with a low centre of gravity, like lots of great players."

"Very true, very true," Archie agreed. "Take Alex James, the great Arsenal playmaker, for example."

"And Maradona," said Zak, who knew a lot about football facts and figures. "He was short and stocky and my dad says he was the best player in the world when Argentina last won the World Cup."

"Indeed," said Archie. He wrinkled his enormous moustache. "However, that still

doesn't make me think any better of moles
. . . To me they are like bad referees."

"Moles aren't like referees!" the twins
exclaimed together.

"Indeed they are," Archie corrected
them.

"But how?" Dan enquired.

"Well," said Archie, "they are blind,
useless and a menace to all around them."

Most of the children laughed, but Sam
screwed up her freckly nose in distaste.

"Well, I think, Archie," she said sharply,
"that you're making a mountain out of a
molehill."

"Ah, you won't say that when this whole
pitch is covered in bumps," Archie insisted,
"and the ball is bobbling about like a buoy
in a hurricane." He raised one pale, bony
finger. "No, if this continues, something will
have to be done. We cannot have our cup
match ruined by a bumpy playing field."

"We could get them with our catapults,"
Giles suggested.

"Yes," added Justin. "Or with my super-
soaker water gun."

"Don't you dare!" said Sam angrily. "You leave them alone." She glowered at the twins, then turned towards Archie and Dan, both of whom were smiling. "I think you're horrible!" she exploded. Then she stormed away across the meadow.

Chapter Three
SAM IN A SULK

The match against Marchmont Road Juniors turned out to be harder than Leggs United had anticipated. The visitors had acquired some good players since the teams had last played and they were much stronger. In addition, with Sam still sulking and hardly getting involved in the game at all, Leggs United were a lot weaker. At half-time, the score was nil–all, but Marchmont had had the better chances. Two fine saves by Gabby and a header off the line by Dan were all that had kept the scoresheet blank.

During the half-time break, Sam refused

to speak to anyone. She sat on her own away from the rest of the team. She wouldn't even talk to her mum or dad.

"Come on, Sam, this is stupid," Dan pleaded, but Sam ignored him.

"Leave her be, laddy," Archie advised. "She'll come round." Herbert Chapman, Archie told his captain, had had countless rows with his great playmaker, Alex James, but it had always worked out all right in the end. On one occasion before an important cup tie, he recalled, the great manager had had to haul his star player out of bed to get him to play. "But patience is a great virtue in these instances," he declared with a small twitch of his moustache.

Dan's patience with his sister was sorely tried in the second half. She didn't like tackling at the best of times, but against Marchmont she made no attempt at all to win the ball. Time after time the opposing midfield players ran past her unchallenged. Dan and his fellow defenders had to work really hard to cover for her.

What really annoyed Dan, though, was

that even when he gave Sam the ball, she didn't use it properly. Normally, she was brilliant on the ball: she dribbled past opponents and passed cleverly. She was, in Archie's words, "the fulcrum of the team", the creator of most of Leggs United's attacks.

There was one move in particular that Archie liked to employ. It was based on a classic Arsenal tactic devised by Herbert Chapman, in which the ball was moved from defence to midfield to the wing and back in to the central striker in a matter of seconds. Leggs United had used the tactic successfully often in their matches so far. But in the game against Marchmont, the move never got going, thanks to Sam. In fact she didn't play a decent pass in the whole match. She kept trying to run with the ball on her own.

Finally, with a quarter of an hour left, matters came to a head. Dan passed the ball to Sam just outside his own penalty area and, half-heartedly, she tried to go past two opponents. They robbed her easily and bore down on the Leggs United goal. Dan and his defenders were outnumbered. The ball was passed among the attacking Marchmont players and found one of their strikers unmarked on the edge of the six-yard box. Fortunately for Leggs United, his shot was a bad one. The ball seemed to take a bobble as he hit it and his shot rolled against the post and behind for a goal kick.

Dan was furious. "Look, if you're going to give the ball away like that, you might as well get off the pitch!" he shouted at Sam, his round face red with anger.

Sam glared back. "OK then, I will!" she shouted. "See how you get on without me." She turned and started to walk from the pitch.

In a flash, Archie was there beside her. "Come on, laddy – I mean lassy," he quickly corrected himself. "You can't desert your team now. They need you."

"No they don't," Sam retorted sharply. "Dan just said so."

"You mustn't take to heart what's said in the heat of the moment," Archie persisted, flashing his young relative a gleaming smile. He flourished his moustache indulgently. "Why, I remember the Arsenal skipper, Herbie Roberts, giving Alex James a terrible earful and . . ."

But Sam butted in before he could get any further. "I don't give a stuff about your old players, Archie," she snapped harshly. "I'm not playing any more and that's final."

And, for the second time that day, she stormed from the meadow.

Chapter Four
GRUMPS AND GRUDGES

Somehow, through desperate defending and a piece of skilful finishing by Zak, a ten-man Leggs United managed to beat Marchmont by one goal to nil. However, the atmosphere at No. 15 Poplar Street, in the days that followed, was far from happy. Dan and Sam were not speaking to one another – and if Sam spoke to anyone else it was usually with a grunt or a snarl.

Sam was especially snappy with the twins, whose latest hobby, playing the recorder, was driving her crazy. Dan had some sympathy with her over this: he found their playing unbearable too. It wasn't just that they were very bad and very loud, it was that they each played a different tune. The cacophony that came from their room was ten times worse than an alley full of fighting tomcats. It certainly did nothing to improve harmony in the Legg household.

Ann and Stephen Legg did their best to smooth things over, so too did Zak, but without success. Dan was willing to make

up with his sister if she made the first move, but there seemed no chance of that. Sam was set into a major sulk.

She wasn't the only one either. Archie was also in a grump. When Dan summoned him from the ball, he smouldered and flickered like hot ashes. He would not speak to Sam, he said, until she apologized to him for her rudeness.

"Herbert Chapman was never treated like this," he declared moodily.

"But I thought you said he often had rows with Alex James," Dan reminded his ghostly ancestor.

"Ah, yes, well," Archie mumbled, "that was different. Alex James was a great star. Your sister's . . . well . . ." He wrinkled his moustache critically. "She's just a temperamental . . . girl."

"Don't I know it," sighed Dan bitterly. He was glad, though, that Sam wasn't in the room to hear Archie's remark. Sparks really would have flown.

It was a difficult few days for Leggs United. The feud between Sam and Dan

and Archie disrupted the team's prep-
arations for their important cup match
against Amberley Park. Archie refused to
hold any training sessions until everything
was sorted out. He wouldn't even discuss
tactics with his team.

"But, Archie, you're our coach," Dan
protested, "and this is our biggest match yet.
We need you."

"Coach I may be, whipping boy I am
not," Archie sniffed. "You can tell your
sister that."

Dan looked at his phantom relative in
bewilderment. "But I don't even know what
it means," he said, tugging at one ear.

Archie drew himself up and glowered at
his captain. "It means that I will not be
spoken to as your sister spoke to me," he
pronounced huffily. Then, quick as a mole
down a hole, he vanished into the old ball.

The following afternoon, after school,
Dan and Zak went down to the meadow to
practise. It seemed odd, though, not having
Sam there too. Dan even missed her jibes
about his shooting ability. The truth was, he

wasn't the sort to hold grudges and his anger with Sam soon passed. He actually felt quite sorry for her. It was a shame that she wasn't going with him and his cousins to meet the Muddington Rovers players – especially as she was such a big fan of Tommy Banks.

By Tuesday evening, he decided that something just had to be done.

"We can't let this go on any longer," he told Zak, as the two of them walked back from the meadow. "We've got to get Archie and Sam talking to one another again or we won't be properly prepared for Saturday's match."

"But how are we going to do that?" Zak asked, his face hidden behind curly strands of black hair.

"I don't know," Dan confessed with a sigh, "but if Sam's still sulking when I get back from school tomorrow, then I'm going up to her room and I'm not going to leave until she's seen sense." He frowned grimly and, remembering Archie's story about Herbert Chapman hauling Alex James out of bed, he added decisively, "I'm going to get her back out on the pitch, even if I have to drag her!"

Chapter Five

MR BARNARD'S BOMBSHELL

By the time Dan returned from school with Zak the next afternoon, Sam's grump seemed the least of his worries. Something had happened that made everything else fade from his mind. Mr Barnard had dropped a bombshell . . .

"Whatever's the matter?" Ann Legg asked, seeing the look of dejection on Dan and Zak's faces. "You two look awful."

"We've had some bad news," said Dan.

"Terrible," sighed Zak. The two boys dropped their sports bags on the hall floor, as if they were discarding all hope.

"Well, come into the sitting room and tell me about it," Ann Legg cajoled.

Dan called up Archie, so that he could hear the bad news too.

"Mr Barnard has arranged an away trip for Saturday afternoon," Dan revealed wretchedly. "It's at some private school down near the coast. Apparently the football teacher there is a friend of his. He had a little tournament planned, but one of the teams had to pull out at the last moment, so he asked Mr Barnard if Muddington Primary would step in." Dan scowled. "I reckon old Barnard only wants to go to show off to his mate about going to the cup game against Tottenham."

Archie peered at Dan with a puzzled air. "This is all very interesting," he muttered, "but I fail to see the problem. You are already playing in a match on Saturday against Amberley Park. Your Mr Barnyard–"

"Barnard," Dan corrected him.

"Your Mr Barnard," Archie continued, "will simply have to replace you and Zak and Zoe with three reserves."

Dan and Zak looked at each other and sighed. "It's not that simple, Archie," Dan informed his phantom ancestor. "We told Barnard about our game, didn't we, Zak?"

Zak nodded in a flurry of ringlets. "We did," he confirmed. "He said we had to play. The school comes first, he said."

"If we don't play, we can't go to the match on Sunday," Dan added glumly.

"Well, that's not right," said Ann Legg sharply. "I'll have a word with him."

But Dan quickly shook his head. "There's no point, Mum," he said hopelessly. "He won't change his mind. He never does."

"Even when he's totally wrong," Zak remarked with unusual bite.

"Like now," said Dan.

"Hmm," Archie muttered with deep disapproval. "He sounds like a very poor manager indeed. The ability to admit one's mistakes is an essential requirement of good management."

The two children looked a little quizzically at their own manager: they'd never heard him admit he was wrong about anything.

"He isn't a good manager," said Dan. He shrugged, then tugged disconsolately at his ear. "But that's not the point. He's *our* manager and what he says goes." He puffed out his round cheeks with a resigned air. "So either we play for Leggs United against Amberley Park and don't go to the match against Tottenham and meet all the Muddington Rovers players . . ." He paused and sighed. "Or we don't play against Amberley, go with the school team on Saturday instead and see the match on Sunday."

"A dilemma indeed," Archie mused, caressing his moustache with great care.

"Well, we've already decided what we're going to do, haven't we, Zak?" Dan said gloomily.

Zak nodded. "We talked about it on the way home from school," he said.

"What *are* you going to do?" Ann Legg enquired.

"We're going to play against Amberley Park, of course," Dan replied limply. "We couldn't let our family down."

It was a noble gesture, but neither Zak or Dan looked any the better for making it. In football-speak, they looked as sick as parrots.

"Well," Dan continued wearily, "I guess I'd better go and talk to Sam. At least she's got one less reason to be grumpy with me now, hasn't she?" He smiled grimly, but as he walked out of the room, his eyes were near to tears.

Chapter Six
LEGGS REUNITED!

Dan knocked on Sam's door, his spirits drooping even further as he read the handwritten sign that hung from the door: *No boys allowed. Keep out! By order. Sam.*

"Who is it?" came the sharp response from the other side of the door.

"It's me, Dan," said Dan softly. "I want to talk to you."

"Well, I don't want to talk to you," Sam retorted sharply. "Go away."

Dan opened the door anyway.

"I said go away!" Sam hissed as Dan walked into her room. Dan stood by the door and gazed in at his sister. She was lying on her bed, reading a football magazine. Next to her on the wall was a huge, full-colour poster of Tommy Banks.

"I'm not going away, Sam," Dan insisted. "Not until we've talked."

Sam sighed heavily and shrugged. "Go on, then," she said coolly. "What have you got to say?"

Dan pulled at his ear tensely. "Well, first, I wanted to say sorry," he began, "for shouting at you in the match on Saturday."

"Huh," Sam grunted. She scowled at the magazine in front of her.

"Sam," Dan pleaded, "we've got to all pull together, otherwise we'll never have a chance against Amberley. We'll go out of the cup in the first round."

"I don't care," Sam growled. But Dan knew she did really. She wanted Leggs United to do well in the cup more than anybody. He suddenly felt a surge of anger: he'd had enough of all this.

"Look, Sam, I'm giving up going to the Tottenham match to play against

Amberley," he exploded. "The least you can do is make up with me and Archie."

Sam was about to respond, then stopped. She stared at Dan quizzically.

"What do you mean, you're giving up the Tottenham match?" she asked.

Dan explained about Mr Barnard's bombshell and what he and Zak had decided to do.

"That's so unfair," Sam said, her own grievances forgotten now. "He can't stop you from going to the match."

"He can," Dan answered miserably. "He has."

He looked so downcast that Sam searched desperately for something to say that might cheer him up. "You could sit with us," she suggested tentatively. "Dad'll get you tickets."

But Dan shook his head. "There aren't any tickets left now," he replied unhappily. "The game's sold out – I heard them say so on the radio this morning."

Now Sam's face fell too. "I'm sorry, Dan," she said.

"Yeah," Dan grunted. He looked down at the floor, his throat tightening, and breathed deeply.

When he felt calmer, he turned again to the reason he'd come to Sam's room. "So . . . you'll play on Saturday? Properly, I mean. You'll be our fulcrum again. Our Alex James."

Sam smiled. "The great Alex James!" she declared in a voice that imitated Archie. Then she and Dan both laughed.

"Archie's still sulking, you know," Dan said. "He hasn't forgiven you for telling him to stuff his old players. He's taken it as a personal insult."

Sam wrinkled her small nose. "I didn't mean it like that," she said. "I was just angry, that's all."

"I know," said Dan. "But could you tell Archie that? We need him to start coaching us again. Things are getting really desperate."

Sam flicked back her fringe and nodded. "Oh, OK," she sighed.

"He's downstairs now, with Zak," Dan

said. He glanced at the door to suggest they go and see. Sam put down her magazine and rolled off the bed. As she did so, a terrible squeaking started up along the landing. The twins had begun their evening recorder practice.

Sam and Dan looked at one another and shook their heads, wincing at the awful combination of Hot Cross Buns and Jingle Bells.

They found Archie, with his foot on the old ball, in the middle of a story about an ancient FA Cup Final. He glanced towards

Sam and Dan as they entered the room, but continued with his tale. As ever it involved Herbert Chapman. He was manager of Huddersfield Town at the time, apparently, and they were playing Preston in the final.

"As I was saying," Archie intoned, with a nod at Zak, "it was a dreadfully dull match until the 67th minute, when Huddersfield were awarded a penalty. Hamilton, the Preston full-back, brought down Billy Smith, the Huddersfield winger, on the edge of the penalty area. But was it inside or outside? Most people thought the latter, but the referee disagreed. 'Penalty!' he said."

Archie paused for a moment and, though he ignored Dan and Sam, Dan could tell he was pleased that his audience had now trebled in size. "The goalkeeper was one JF Mitchell," Archie continued with a disapproving twitch of his great moustache, "and he danced about on his line like an excited monkey begging for peanuts. It was quite ridiculous." His hairy eyebrows met in an upside-down V.

"I've heard of him," Zak said.

"Indeed?" Archie queried with a gratified smile.

"He's the only goalie to wear glasses in a cup final," Zak stated proudly.

"Quite right," Archie congratulated his young relative, "he did wear glasses. But he didn't save the penalty. Smith scored and Huddersfield won the cup." Archie beamed at the memory.

"Another great day for Herbert Chapman, eh?" Dan ventured lightly.

Archie looked at Dan. "A good day certainly," he agreed. "Though, of course, his best days were yet to come."

"At Arsenal," Zak affirmed.

"Precisely," Archie nodded.

"With Alex James," Sam interjected. Then, having got the phantom coach's attention, she added quickly, "I'm sorry for what I said the other day, Archie. Really I am. I was angry with Dan, not you. I know Alex James was a great player."

"Hmm," Archie muttered. His eyebrows hopped and his moustache wiggled, as he regarded his young playmaker. "Well, apology accepted," he declared at last. "Now we can commence with planning our own cup victory – once we've sorted out this other unfortunate matter, of course . . ."

Sam's eyes sparked with outrage. "It's not right!" she cried suddenly. She gestured towards Dan and Zak. "You were invited to the Tottenham match. You should be allowed to go."

"Try telling old Barnard that," Dan commented bitterly.

There was silence for a moment, then Archie gave a small cough. In the twilight, his ghostly figure gleamed and shimmered. "Well," he announced decisively, "that is precisely what I intend to do."

Chapter Seven
GHOST AT SCHOOL

The next morning, Archie accompanied the children to school.

"But, Archie," Dan protested, "Mr Barnard won't be able to hear you if you do talk to him."

Archie, it had been established, was only visible and audible to his own family – a state of affairs that had already caused him much frustration. Today, however, he was nonchalance itself, as he floated along the street, his outline glowing brightly.

"Ah, trust me," he said mysteriously, tapping one bony finger to his nose. "We spirits have ways of making ourselves understood."

"If you say so," Dan said with a despondent air. He didn't hold out much hope that Archie would be successful. He felt doomed to missing out on being a guest of honour at the Tottenham match.

When they arrived at school, Archie went with Dan, Zak and Zoe towards their classroom.

"Good luck," Sam called as they walked away.

"Luck?" Archie retorted with an extravagant waggle of his huge moustache. "Who needs luck, laddy, when you have genius?"

Sam smiled and shook her head. "I hope you're right, Archie," she said to herself.

As he floated through the school, Archie had plenty to say about what he saw around him. For a start, there was the uniform. When he was a lad, he remarked, ties and blazers were obligatory – he didn't approve of the sweatshirts and tracksuit trousers that many of the children wore. But it was their shoes that drew his greatest criticism.

"In my day," he stated sternly, "you could see your face in your shoes, they were so shiny." He glanced down proudly at the gleaming toecaps of his own size-twelve boots. "I always kept my footwear in immaculate condition," he added, looking pointedly at Dan's shoes, which were scuffed and dull.

"My dad polishes my shoes once a week," Dan said defensively.

"Once a week, laddy!" Archie exclaimed. "Shoes should be polished every day. You should treat them like you treat your pet rabbit."

"But I don't have a pet rabbit," Dan replied, bemused.

"Well, all the more reason to look after your shoes," Archie insisted.

But if he was critical of the pupils' dress, Archie was horrified at their teachers' appearance.

"Why, I've seen smarter tramps," he sniffed disgustedly as they passed a group of teachers in the corridor. The children burst out laughing – then quickly had to pretend they were coughing when the teachers glared at them.

They came at last to the top classroom. Dan, Zak and Zoe sat at their tables, while Archie prowled about the room peering reproachfully about him. When Mr Barnard came in, Archie fixed him with a steely gaze.

"So this is your manager," he observed dismissively.

As the teacher read the register, Archie wandered to the front of the class. He studied Mr Barnard closely. "Well, at least he's wearing a jacket and tie," he commented. He ran one finger lightly across the teacher's collar. "Limp," he scolded. "Not nearly enough starch."

Mr Barnard paused and glanced up from his book with a puzzled expression. He waggled his neck as if to get rid of some minor irritation.

Zak and Zoe stared at Archie goggle-eyed, while Dan frowned and shook his head vigorously.

"Is something the matter, Daniel?" Mr Barnard demanded sharply.

Dan froze. "No, sir," he muttered. "My neck was just a bit stiff."

"Mmm," the teacher murmured. "I trust it'll unstiffen by Saturday. You are coming with us on Saturday, aren't you?" He gave Dan a piercing look.

Dan's head bowed; his heart thumped in his chest. "No, sir," he said quietly.

"No?" Mr Barnard queried. His small, deep-set eyes bored into Dan, who shuffled on his chair uneasily.

"I can't go on the school trip, sir," Dan explained. "I've got to play for Leggs United."

"Really?" Mr Barnard snorted. "And what about you, Zak? And Zoe?"

The two children shook their heads. "We have to play for Leggs United too," Zak said.

"Very well. But you know the consequences," Mr Barnard informed them. "If you don't come with the team on Saturday, you don't come on Sunday either." He raised his hands. "Right, that's my last word on the subject. Now, let's get on." He picked up his pen to continue, but Archie tapped it from his fingers. The pen rolled across the teacher's desk and clattered on to the floor.

"Now, just a minute, sir," Archie remonstrated. He loomed over Mr Barnard like a huge flame. "This matter is far from closed. These lads are playing for me on Saturday and you have no right to punish them." He raised a finger like a referee giving a caution. "I demand that you reverse your decision," he boomed.

It was an impressive performance, but

wasted of course. Mr Barnard neither saw nor heard Archie. He picked up his pen and, after studying it a moment, he completed the register.

"Right, class, maths books out," he ordered.

But Archie was far from finished. When Mr Barnard got up and began to walk around the tables, Archie sat down in his seat and started writing. When Mr Barnard returned to his desk, he looked down and frowned. Waves of deep wrinkles appeared on his large forehead and his eyes looked hostile.

"Daniel," he said. "I presume this is your work." He held up a piece of paper and read it out: "*Dan, Zak and Zoe must be allowed to play for Leggs United on Saturday without penalty. Signed, Archibald Legg, the Phantom of the Cup.*"

"The Phantom of the Cup," Mr Barnard repeated tartly. He glared at Dan. "Save your imagination for creative writing, Daniel. Any more nonsense like this and I shall put you in detention this lunchtime."

"But it wasn't me, sir," Dan complained.

"Oh, I suppose it really was a ghost, was it?" Mr Barnard mocked.

Dan's body sagged. What was the point of trying to explain? Mr Barnard would never believe him.

Archie attempted to come to his young relative's assistance.

"Leave the boy be," he rebuked, his eyes ablaze. "It was I, Archibald Legg, who wrote the note." As before, however, his words fell on deaf ears.

For a while, Archie retreated to the windowsill, where he perched like some massive bird, deep in thought. But he was determined to make himself "heard", and he was soon up on his feet again.

His next trick was truly spectacular. While Mr Barnard was rummaging in a big storage cupboard and the children were busy with their maths, Archie picked up a piece of chalk and started writing on the blackboard, repeating his earlier message.

Gradually faces started to turn towards the blackboard and an astonished gasp went round the room at the sight of a piece of chalk writing on its own.

Mr Barnard was the last to witness Archie's display. He appeared from the cupboard with a box of maths puzzles, just as Archie was signing his name. The teacher gaped, eyes boggling, for an instant, his face draining of colour. He swallowed so hard that his Adam's apple bounced in his throat. The box of puzzles dropped from his hands and spilled noisily across the floor . . .

The racket seemed to snap him out of his stupor. He turned to Dan with a furious expression.

"I don't know how you did that, Daniel," he thundered, "but you can spend your lunch hour in here, writing that message until you're as sick of the sight of it as I am!"

Dan closed his eyes in silent misery. Archie's antics had made things much worse, not better. The situation was hopeless.

Chapter Eight
BAD NEWS AND GOOD

Dan was the picture of gloom that afternoon as he told his family about his disastrous day at school – and Archie's part in it.

"Where is Archie?" Sam asked when he'd finished.

Dan shrugged. "Back in his ball, I suppose," he said. "He disappeared at the end of school."

"He's probably too embarrassed to show his face," Ann Legg remarked drily, "after the mess he seems to have made of things." She ruffled Dan's hair comfortingly. "This whole business is very unfair," she said. "I really think I ought to speak to Mr Barnard."

Dan shook his head at once. "No, Mum, please," he begged. "There's no point." He sighed. "Besides, he's already said that if there's any more trouble, he'll drop me from the school team."

"Well, if you insist," Ann Legg agreed reluctantly. "But Julia will have a word with him, I'm sure." Julia Browne, Zak's mum, was a teacher at Muddington Primary.

"She won't," Dan said. "Zak's asked her not to."

After tea, Dan went round to the Brownes' to see his cousin. Sam, mean- while, decided to call up Archie. It was his duty to sort things out, she reckoned. If he was such a genius then he ought to do something to prove it, not skulk away inside that old pig's bladder that he inhabited.

"Archie!" she wailed, gently rubbing the football. "Arise, O Archie!"

But nothing happened.

She tried once more, with the same

result. Archie, it seemed, had not yet returned from his outing to school.

Before going to bed that evening, Sam made another attempt to summon Archie, but again without success. She looked anxiously at the old football in her hands. *I hope he knows the way back*, she thought. Then she wondered if ghosts could get lost. For an instant, she imagined herself putting up one of the notices that she'd seen on trees: *Missing, black and white kitten named Fluffykins.* Only her notice would read: *Missing, phantom footballer named Archie . . .* No one could see him, though, so they wouldn't be able to help find him, would they? She went to bed feeling quite concerned about her ghostly relative.

Archie still hadn't returned next morning when Sam tried once more to summon him. She told Dan of his continued absence on the way to school.

"Oh, that's all we need," Dan groaned. "The day before our first ever cup match and our coach goes missing." He looked so glum that Sam decided not to mention her worries that Archie might actually be lost.

What seemed like further bad news awaited Dan on his arrival at school. He was to go at once to the office of Mrs Samuels, the head teacher. "What now?" he wailed.

"Perhaps she's heard what's happened to you and wants to talk about it," Sam suggested hopefully. Then, less hopefully, she added, "She might be on your side."

"Yeah, and pigs might fly," Dan muttered darkly.

He went off to his interview with a face like stewed rhubarb.

Yet when Sam next saw him, at morning break, he was grinning like Christmas Day! Beside him, Zak and Zoe were grinning too.

"What is it?" she cried, unable to believe her eyes. "What's happened?"

"It's all sorted!" Dan yelled and he gave his sister a great hug.

"Oi, you're crushing me!" Sam spluttered laughingly.

Dan released his grip and put his arms round Zak and Zoe. "We're go-o-ing to

Wembley. We're go-o-ing to Wembley," he crooned happily.

"You're going to Wembley?" Sam quizzed incredulously.

Dan laughed. "Well, we're going to Muddington Rovers against Tottenham anyway," he crowed. Then he explained how his fortunes had turned around so dramatically.

The summons to Mrs Samuels' office had not been to receive further bad news – quite the contrary. Mr Barnard had phoned in sick that morning. He'd sounded very shaky

indeed, the head teacher had said. However, he had been very concerned that a message should be given to Dan. It was this: Dan, Zak and Zoe were excused the school team trip the next day. Indeed it seemed likely that the whole trip would be cancelled, Mrs Samuels had said, for Mr Barnard had sounded in a terrible state.

"But can we go to the Muddington Rovers game on Sunday?" Dan had implored the head teacher anxiously.

"Yes, of course," Mrs Samuels had assured him. "Mr Barnard was quite particular about that. 'Tell them, I shall see them on Sunday,' he said." Then she had sent Dan back to his classroom.

"So that's it! Everything's going to be all right after all!" Dan rejoiced.

"Why do you think he changed his mind?" asked Zak.

"Who cares!" said Dan. He started singing again and, this time, Zak and Zoe joined in.

Sam watched them, a broad smile on her freckly face.

But then a dark cloud blotted her sunshine. Everything wasn't yet all right, was it? Archie! What had happened to Archie?

Chapter Nine
ARCHIE GOES A-HAUNTING

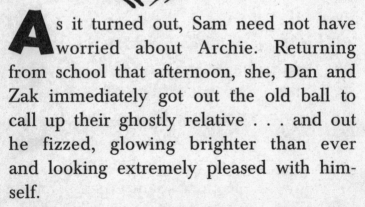

As it turned out, Sam need not have worried about Archie. Returning from school that afternoon, she, Dan and Zak immediately got out the old ball to call up their ghostly relative . . . and out he fizzed, glowing brighter than ever and looking extremely pleased with himself.

"Greetings, lads!" he declaimed heartily. "I take it that all is well."

"Archie!" Sam exclaimed. "Where on earth have you been?"

"I have been a-haunting," he replied

mysteriously. "But first, have you any news to tell me?"

Excitedly Dan told Archie all about his meeting with Mrs Samuels and the good tidings she had given him.

"I don't know what made old Barnard change his mind," Dan concluded with a shrug. "But he did, that's the important thing."

Archie's moustache waggled with amusement. "I think I might know what made Mr Barnard change his mind," he gloated.

The three children gazed hard at their phantom manager.

"Archie!" Sam cried. "It was you!"

"What did you do?" Dan enquired.

"I merely made your teacher see the error of his ways," Archie replied teasingly.

"Come on, Archie!" Sam urged. "Tell us what happened, please!"

"Very well," Archie intoned suavely. "Sit down and all shall be revealed."

There was nothing Archie liked better than relating a story to an attentive audience

– and no audience could have been more attentive than Sam, Zak and Dan. They listened, completely enthralled, as he told them of his exploits the evening before.

Having failed to make the desired impression on Mr Barnard at school, Archie had decided he would have to follow his fellow manager home and there indulge in some serious haunting. It wasn't something he'd done much of, he explained, which is why his efforts in the classroom had not been more successful.

"Once I entered your Mr Barnard's

house, however, I soon mastered the technique," he said proudly. "And then, though I say it myself, I was rather good."

Usually these statements of self-praise brought groans from the children, but on this occasion they were too eager to hear what Archie had to say to interrupt.

"I began with some simple tricks," Archie continued. "Mr Barnard hung up his coat. I knocked it off its peg and on to the floor. He picked it up, I knocked it off. And so it went on, up and down, for some minutes, until he became irritated and I grew bored. Then we went into the kitchen, where the real fun began." Archie paused, radiant at the memory. "I opened cupboard doors, he closed them. I opened them again. He closed them. I opened them – and so on. Then I chucked a few things about the room, as we ghosts are wont to do."

"What sort of things?" Dan asked, tugging on his ear.

"Oh, you know, rice, sugar, eggs, that sort of thing," Archie replied casually.

"Wow!" Sam exclaimed.

"Cool," said Zak.

"By now, he seemed a little perturbed," Archie continued, "but still not sufficiently agitated, I felt. So I emptied a bag of flour over his head."

"You emptied a bag of flour over Mr Barnard's head?" Dan gawked.

"Indeed I did," Archie nodded. "Just to let him know I was there, to get his attention."

"I bet you did that all right," laughed Sam.

Archie raised one bushy eyebrow. "It seemed to do the trick," he confirmed. "Then I delivered my message. It was the same one I had expressed in the classroom, but, one to one, its effect was considerably more powerful – particularly as I wrote it in the spilled flour." Archie beamed at his young relatives. "A nice touch, I thought," he added.

Archie had haunted Mr Barnard all night long. He had pursued him around the house, tripped him up and snatched things from his grasp. When the teacher had tried to hide in bed, Archie had tipped up the mattress and pulled the pillow out from beneath his head. And everywhere – in flour, in ink, even in the condensation on the windows – Archie had written his message: *Dan, Zak and Zoe must be allowed to play for Leggs United on Saturday without penalty. Signed, Archibald Legg, the Phantom of the Cup.*

"It seems to have got through to him, eventually," Archie concluded with a flourish of his walrus moustache.

"Archie, you're a genius," Dan declared exuberantly. "You really are."

"Laddy, laddy," Archie retorted nonchalantly, "tell me something I do not already know."

Chapter Ten
WRONG-FOOTED

Number 15 Poplar Street was a happy, noisy house on Saturday morning. There was a real buzz of excitement in anticipation of the weekend's cup games. Practising on their recorders, the twins even managed to play the same melody at the same time – and almost in tune. It seemed, to Sam and Dan, like a good omen for what was to come.

There was only one minor hiccup: the state of the meadow. The moles had been busy again during the night and there were a number of bumps on the pitch. Sam and

Dan discovered them when they went down for a kickabout after breakfast.

"If Archie sees these molehills, he'll do his nut," Dan remarked, with an anxious pull on his ear.

"You're telling me," Sam agreed, flicking back her fringe. "We'll just have to make sure he doesn't see them," she stated decisively.

"How are we going to do that?" Dan asked.

"Like this," Sam cried, and she leapt with both feet on to one of the molehills. Then she leapt again. "We'll flatten them," she laughed, stamping.

"I thought you liked moles," Dan teased.

"Well, I do," Sam declared. "But I don't want to play on a pitch covered in bumps. Anyway, we're not actually hurting the moles."

Dan followed his sister's lead and soon Zak and the twins appeared and joined in as well. Flattening the molehills turned into a fun game. The five children leapt about the meadow like giant, jet-powered frogs. It was tiring too. After a while, they all collapsed

in the middle of the pitch and lay on their backs in the late summer sunshine.

"That was cool," Zak commented and, noisily, the twins agreed.

"Good fitness training too," Dan observed breathlessly.

"And we got rid of all the bumps," Sam said contentedly.

Their efforts did not go unappreciated, when Archie inspected the pitch later, just before the kick-off against Amberley Park.

"There are a few blemishes, I see," he remarked with a slight twitch of his moustache. "But all in all, the surface seems to be in reasonable condition." He turned to his team with a serious expression. "I shall expect great football from you this afternoon," he said gravely. "Remember this is the cup. A draw is no use. To progress, we must win. Let's make this a memorable weekend: a victory for Leggs United in the cup today; a victory for Muddington Rovers tomorrow." He paused, before continuing in a lighter tone, "As the great Herbert Chapman once said, 'All good things come in twos.' "

The children laughed.

"You made that up," Dan accused the phantom footballer.

"Well, perhaps I did," Archie confessed and his eyebrows hopped playfully. "Still, it's rather good, don't you think?"

Dan and Sam looked at each other and groaned.

Amberley Park were a strong team. They were high in the league like Leggs United and had only lost once away from home. Watching them line up in their yellow and black striped shirts, Dan regretted all the training sessions his team had missed that week. He hoped they wouldn't be made to pay for their lack of preparation. In any case, he felt pretty sure he was in for another busy afternoon.

In fact, during the first half, both defences were busy. The match was end to end, one side attacking and then the other. The main threat posed by Amberley came from their right-winger, a tall, tricky player called Tom. A couple of times early in the game, he took on Justin and went past him on the outside. Fortunately for Leggs United, his crosses were not very accurate and were easily cleared. As the half went on, however, the winger changed his line of attack to come inside Justin on the defender's right foot, which was his weaker one by a long way.

The first time the Amberley winger adopted the tactic, he completely surprised Dan and his fellow defenders. Darting easily past Justin, Tom found himself in the Leggs United area with a clear run on goal.

He took full advantage. Sprinting forward, he slipped the ball past the advancing keeper, Gabby, into the bottom corner of the goal. Amberley Park were in the lead.

But their lead didn't last long. In keeping with the game so far, Leggs United went on the attack from the restart and forced a corner. Sam swung the ball in from the right with her left foot, Rollo Browne flicked the ball on at the near post and Zoe headed it into the top of the net. She lost her glasses in the process, but she didn't care. She stood in the Amberley goalmouth, grinning sort of woozily, until Zak returned her glasses. Then she ran back to her own half with her arms in the air, whooping like a hyena. It was her first ever goal for Leggs United.

On the touchline, Ann and Stephen Legg, Mark and Nadya Legg, and Julia and Otis Browne applauded wildly and shouted encouragement. Beside them, Archie allowed himself a small, indulgent smile, while his outline shone like polished silver.

It was Amberley Park and their winger,

Tom, who had the last laugh, though – at least in the first half. Only minutes after Zak had hit the inside of the visitors' post, the ball was played out to the Amberley right. Tom took the ball in his stride and ran at Justin. He dummied to go outside the full-back, then cut inside again. Justin was completely wrong-footed and, once more, Tom was through.

This time, though, Dan had got himself in a better position to cover the winger's run. However, he too was fooled by the winger's trickery. A clever shimmy and the Amberley player had another clear shooting chance. He arrowed the ball into the far corner of the net with Gabby helpless. Amberley Park were ahead again and Leggs United were in trouble.

Chapter Eleven
TWIN SWITCH

Leggs United were still two–one down when they came off at half-time. It had been an even game, though, and they weren't too disheartened. Nor indeed was Archie. He regarded his team thoughtfully.

"For the most part," he contended, "your play has been admirable." He gazed down at the diagram of Arsenal's famous ten-second wonder goal that was painted on the grass next to the pitch. "At least," he added, "your attacking play has been good. Defensively, we have a problem."

"That winger's brilliant," Dan declared.

"He's not bad," Archie conceded. "He reminds me a little of Cliff Bastin – very cool in front of goal." Cliff Bastin was a fast, goal-scoring winger in Herbert Chapman's Arsenal team. Archie had mentioned him many times and always with the greatest admiration.

"The thing is," Dan worried, "how are we going to stop him?"

"Yes," Sam agreed sharply. "It's no good us scoring goals at their end if he keeps scoring in our goal. We've got to do something." She tossed back her head impetuously.

Archie raised one large, pale hand. "Patience, patience," he soothed. "Am I not Archibald Legg, master tactician?"

"You mean you've got a solution?" Dan asked eagerly.

"Naturally," Archie replied. "For the second half, I intend to make a slight adjustment. The twins, Jules and Dustin–"

"Giles and Justin!" chorused the twins as one.

"Er, quite so," Archie blustered. "Giles

and Justin will switch sides – Giles on the left and Justin on the right."

His announcement was met with blank looks and bewilderment.

"Is that it?" Dan queried, bemused.

"That's it," Archie beamed. "A master-stroke, don't you think?"

The children glanced at one another and shrugged. What on earth was Archie up to?

The brilliance of Archie's plan, however, soon became apparent. In Amberley's first attack of the second half, the ball was quickly fed out to Tom. Without hesitation he ran at his opposing full-back, who was now the right-footed Giles, not the left-footed Justin. As in the first half, Tom feinted to go outside, then stepped inside. But this time, the winger was attacking the full-back's stronger side and Giles easily took the ball off him.

Minutes later, Tom got the ball again and attempted the same manoeuvre, a little quicker this time. But Giles made another strong tackle, winning the ball back for his team, who mounted an attack of their own.

As Leggs United went forward, Tom gazed at Giles with a puzzled expression. Dan could see what he was thinking: How could this full-back, who was so weak on his right foot in the first half, suddenly become so strong on that side now? Dan smiled. The winger obviously hadn't noticed that Leggs United were playing identical twins at full-back.

When, in the visitors' next attack, Giles robbed Tom for a third time with a fine right-footed tackle, the Amberley player shook his head and frowned. He looked completely disheartened. The next time he received the ball, he didn't attempt a run.

He just kicked it back into his own half.

With Tom shackled, Amberley's attacking options were severely weakened. At the other end of the pitch, meanwhile, Leggs United were rampant. On the wings, Frances and Ben, two of the Legg triplets, were causing havoc with their pace. The tiring Amberley full-backs were no match for them. So it was no surprise when, from one of Ben's runs, Zak hit the equalizing goal.

Now the second half became one-way traffic in the direction of the Amberley goal. Prompted by Sam's clever playmaking, Leggs United created several chances: Zak hit a post, Rollo had a shot cleared off the line, Sam herself curled a free-kick just over the bar. Finally, though, Amberley cracked.

It was a move that would have brought a smile to Herbert Chapman's face, as Archie remarked later. Dan won the ball deep in defence. He slid it through to Sam in midfield. She swivelled and swept the ball out to the left flank, halfway inside the Amberley half. Frances sprinted after it, carried the ball forward to the penalty area, before crossing to Zak. He controlled the ball and advanced in one movement, then flicked the ball inside to Ben who raced on to fire an unstoppable drive past the Amberley keeper. Leggs United were in the lead!

The Leggs spectators cheered and hugged one another. This time, even Archie showed his delight. He waved his arms in the air and did a little jig of joy, his knobbly knees pumping comically. Watching him, the twins collapsed in a fit of laughter.

For the rest of the game, Amberley were a beaten side. Their heads went down and they were no match for their exuberant opponents. Zak dribbled past three defenders to score his second goal and Sam completed the rout with a fine run and shot from the edge of the Amberley penalty box.

When the final whistle went, Leggs United had won by five goals to two. Their first ever cup match had ended in a great victory . . .

Now, it was over to Muddington Rovers.

Chapter Twelve
THE BIG MATCH

The atmosphere inside the ground was electric. At each end, rival supporters sang their chants lustily. There was a real sense of expectation amongst the Muddington Rovers crowd that today their team could pull off an amazing giant-killing feat and knock out the mighty Tottenham Hotspur.

In their special seats in the central stand, the Muddington Primary football team chattered excitedly, discussing their recent meeting with the Muddington Rovers players.

Dan gazed down in awe at his programme and the autographs he had collected. All the Muddington Rovers players had signed their names and so too had the Tottenham Hotspur stars. Beside Dan, Archie hovered restlessly in the aisle, looking around with interest and impatience, while in the seat on Dan's other side, Zak sat staring at the pitch, as if he were in a dream. It had all been so amazing.

One member of the party seemed particularly overawed by the occasion. It wasn't a child; it was Mr Barnard. He was very quiet all afternoon and appeared to be uncharacteristically nervous. He kept glancing over his shoulder as if he feared someone was following him – and with some justification, for every now and then Archie did indeed take up a position behind the teacher, looming over him like an avenging angel. Once the phantom footballer even proposed pouring a cup of cold tea over the teacher's head, but Dan dissuaded him.

"I think you've haunted him enough,

Archie," he said firmly. "He's got the message."

"Oh, very well," Archie muttered disappointedly. "I must say I was rather enjoying being a troublesome spook."

"Well, now you can be a spooktator instead," Zak joked.

As they waited for the teams to appear, Archie entertained his young relatives with talk of famous cup upsets of the past – the greatest of which involved Herbert Chapman's Arsenal.

"It was just a year before he died, 1933," Archie stated solemnly. "The press called Arsenal 'The Bank of England', because of all their expensive players, while Walsall, their opponents, were worth just £69. Several influential Arsenal players were unable to play, however, having been laid low with influenza." Archie sighed deeply. "Sadly, their replacements were not up to the mark," he lamented. "Walsall won by two goals to nil."

Archie's expression was so tragic that Dan felt quite sorry for him.

"Oh well," he cajoled. "If the great Arsenal can be beaten like that, then there's hope for Muddington Rovers, isn't there?"

This suggestion appeared to revive Archie's spirits. "You have a point," he conceded, with a small twitch of his big moustache.

As it happened, however, the game began badly for Muddington Rovers. Tottenham Hotspur took the lead with their first attack of the game and, by half-time, they were three goals ahead.

During the interval, Archie decided to join Stephen Legg, Sam and the twins, who were watching the match from behind one of the goals.

"It's good to get an all-round view of the game," he declared coolly, before floating away through the air.

"I bet Sam's in a right strop," Dan remarked, watching Archie go. "Tommy Banks has hardly had a kick."

"Except that one the Tottenham sweeper gave him," observed Zak ruefully.

Dan tugged at his ear anxiously. "He'd

better not get injured," he said. "It would ruin our surprise."

His worries, however, were unfounded. The second half was far more evenly balanced than the first and Tommy Banks played as well as anyone. In fact, to the home crowd's delight, he scored the only goal of the half. With just minutes remaining, he jinked past two Tottenham defenders and thumped the ball into the net. It may only have been a consolation

goal, but the Muddington supporters celebrated as if it were the winner.

At the end of the match, the Muddington Rovers team was given a standing ovation by their fans – Dan, Zak and Zoe among them. The applause continued until the last player had left the pitch.

And then, as the spectators started to leave, came the tannoy's announcement.

Chapter Thirteen
A SPECIAL SURPRISE

"**W**ill Sam Legg please see the steward at Entrance P. He has an important message for her." The announcement resounded around the emptying stadium.

Sam sat bolt upright in her seat with a look of astonishment on her freckly, now pink face. Beside her, hovering in the aisle, Archie raised one bushy eyebrow.

"That's you, Sam!" cried the twins as one.

"It is," Stephen Legg agreed. He looked at his daughter with a wry smile. "Unless there's someone else in this ground with exactly the same name," he teased, "which I doubt very much."

"But what can it be about?" Sam wondered. She peered across at the special area of the central stand where Dan, Zak, Zoe and the rest of the Muddington Primary school team had been seated. But the seats were empty.

"Don't you think you ought to go and find out?" Stephen Legg prompted.

"Go on, Sam!" Justin shouted.

"Hurry up!" Giles urged.

"An excellent idea," Archie agreed. He wrinkled his moustache theatrically. "I shall accompany you."

Entrance P was just above them and, as most of the spectators in their block had departed by now, it took Archie and an excited Sam only moments to get there.

"Sam Legg?" enquired a burly man in a luminous yellow steward's jacket.

Sam nodded. "Yes," she said breathlessly.

"I'm to take you to your brother," the steward informed her. "He needs to speak to you about something."

"What is it?" Sam asked, puzzled.

"I don't know, love," the steward shrugged. "I'm just the messenger."

Sam turned to her ghostly relative. "Come on, Archie!" she urged.

"Eh?" said the steward in obvious confusion.

"Oh, nothing," said Sam quickly, blushing. "I was just talking to my invisible friend."

"Ah," said the steward with an understanding smile. "I used to have one of them. Bobo, I called him."

"Bobo!" Archie repeated disdainfully, as he followed Sam and the steward out of the stand.

They walked along several corridors and down a number of staircases before stopping at last by a door that said: *Private – Hospitality Suite*.

"Well, here we are," the steward said genially.

Sam's heart was racing as the steward opened the door. But it almost galloped away completely when she saw who was in the room beyond, looking straight at her as she walked through the doorway. It was Tommy Banks! Next to him, with a huge grin on his round face, was Dan.

"Surprise, surprise," he grinned.

"Ah, this must be my number one fan," Tommy Banks greeted Sam. "Put it there." He reached out a hand to shake. "It's a pleasure to meet you," he said warmly.

For once, Sam was quite lost for words. She just nodded her head with a shy smile and shook her hero's hand.

"Your brother tells me you wanted my autograph, so I've signed this for you,"

said Tommy Banks. He handed Sam a programme of that day's match against Tottenham. Across the front, he'd written: *To Sam, best wishes. Thanks for your support!* Then he'd signed his name underneath.

"Thanks," Sam muttered, quite overcome.

Tommy Banks winked. "It's the least I could do," he remarked. "Sorry we couldn't manage a win for you."

"That's OK," Sam uttered timidly.

"Well, you can't win 'em all, can you?" Tommy Banks continued heartily. "Unless you're Man. United, of course." He grinned broadly. "Well, I'd better get back to the bath," he laughed, "before the lads take all the hot water." He put his hand on Sam's shoulder for a second, then winked again. "See you. Keep cheering," he said. Then with a quick wave of his hand, he strode away.

Sam watched her hero go, then turned and threw her arms round Dan's neck.

"You're a star," she cried happily.

"It was Tommy Banks's idea," Dan said

modestly. "When I told him how much you adore him, he said he just had to meet you."

Sam snorted.

"He seems a nice enough young fellow," Archie remarked amiably. "Though I still say he could do with losing a few pounds. Now, in my day . . ."

"Oh, Archie, be quiet," Dan said good-humouredly. "Can't you see Sam's in love?"

Sam aimed a playful punch at her brother.

"Hmph," said Archie, his eyebrows hopping like frisky caterpillars. "It takes all sorts, I suppose." He stroked his moustache thoughtfully. "Well, Muddington Rovers may have lost a game, but they've certainly won a heart." He nodded at the still beaming Sam – and, in that joyful moment, the phantom manager shone like the FA Cup itself.

Collect all the **Leggs United** books!

The prices shown below are correct at the time of going to press. However, Macmillan Publishers reserve the right to show new retail prices on covers which may differ from those previously advertised.

ALAN DURANT

1. The Phantom Footballer	0 330 35126 5	£2.99
2. Fair Play or Foul?	0 330 35127 3	£2.99
3. Up for the Cup	0 330 35128 1	£2.99
4. Spot the Ball	0 330 35129 X	£2.99
5. Red Card for the Ref	0 330 35130 3	£2.99
6. Team on Tour	0 330 35131 1	£2.99
7. Sick as a Parrot	0 330 37449 4	£2.99
8. Super Sub	0 330 37450 8	£2.99

All Macmillan titles can be ordered at your local bookshop or are available by post from:

Book Service by Post
PO Box 29, Douglas, Isle of Man IM99 1BQ

Credit cards accepted. For details:
Telephone: 01624 675137
Fax: 01624 670923
E-mail: bookshop@enterprise.net

Free postage and packing in the UK.
Overseas customers: add £1 per book (paperback)
and £3 per book (hardback).